Symbols of American Freedom

The Statue of Liberty

by Mari Schuh

BELLWETHER MEDIA • MINNEAPOLIS, MN

Note to Librarians, Teachers, and Parents:

Blastoff! Readers are carefully developed by literacy experts and combine standards-based content with developmentally appropriate text.

Level 1 provides the most support through repetition of high-frequency words, light text, predictable sentence patterns, and strong visual support.

Level 2 offers early readers a bit more challenge through varied simple sentences, increased text load, and less repetition of high-frequency words.

Level 3 advances early-fluent readers toward fluency through increased text and concept load, less reliance on visuals, longer sentences, and more literary language.

Level 4 builds reading stamina by providing more text per page, increased use of punctuation, greater variation in sentence patterns, and increasingly challenging vocabulary.

Level 5 encourages children to move from "learning to read" to "reading to learn" by providing even more text, varied writing styles, and less familiar topics.

Whichever book is right for your reader, Blastoff! Readers are the perfect books to build confidence and encourage a love of reading that will last a lifetime!

This edition first published in 2019 by Bellwether Media, Inc.

Library of Congress Cataloging-in-Publication Data

Names: Schuh, Mari C., 1975-
Title: The Statue of Liberty / by Mari Schuh.
Description: Minneapolis, MN : Bellwether Media, Inc., 2019. | Series: Blastoff! Readers: Symbols of American Freedom | Includes bibliographical references and index.
Identifiers: LCCN 2017061646 (print) | LCCN 2017061779 (ebook) | ISBN 9781626178878 (hardcover : alk. paper) | ISBN 9781618914736 (pbk. : alk. paper) | ISBN 9781681035505 (ebook)
Subjects: LCSH: Statue of Liberty (New York, N.Y.)–History–Juvenile literature. | New York (N.Y.)–Buildings, structures, etc.–Juvenile literature.
Classification: LCC F128.64.L6 (ebook) | LCC F128.64.L6 S38 2019 (print) | DDC 974.7–dc23
LC record available at https://lccn.loc.gov/2017061646

Editor: Rebecca Sabelko Designer: Andrea Schneider

Printed in the United States of America, North Mankato, MN.

Table of Contents

What Is the Statue of Liberty?

The Statue of Liberty is a **symbol** of **democracy**. Some call it Lady Liberty.

The Statue is in New York **Harbor**. It welcomes people to the United States.

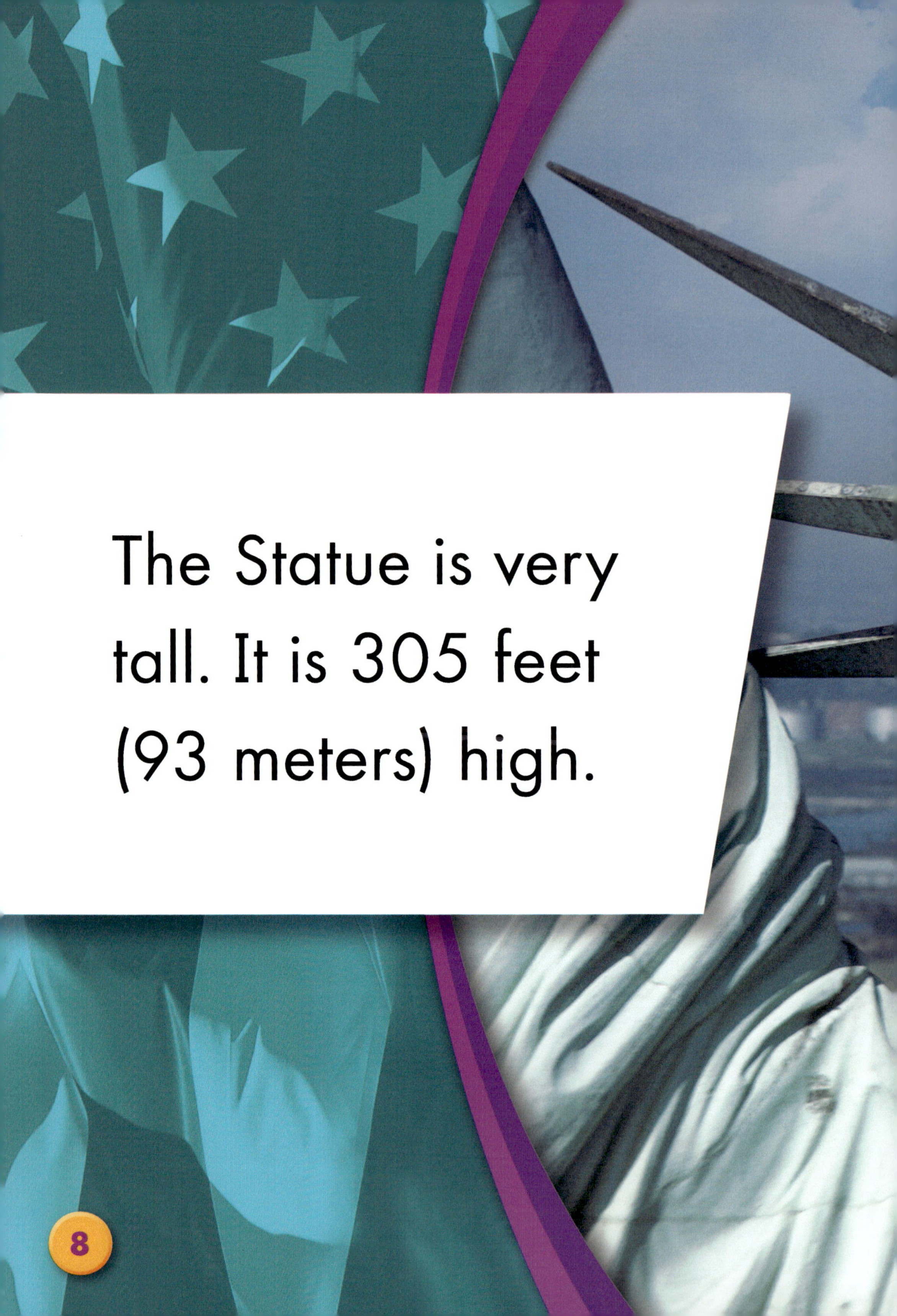

The Statue is very tall. It is 305 feet (93 meters) high.

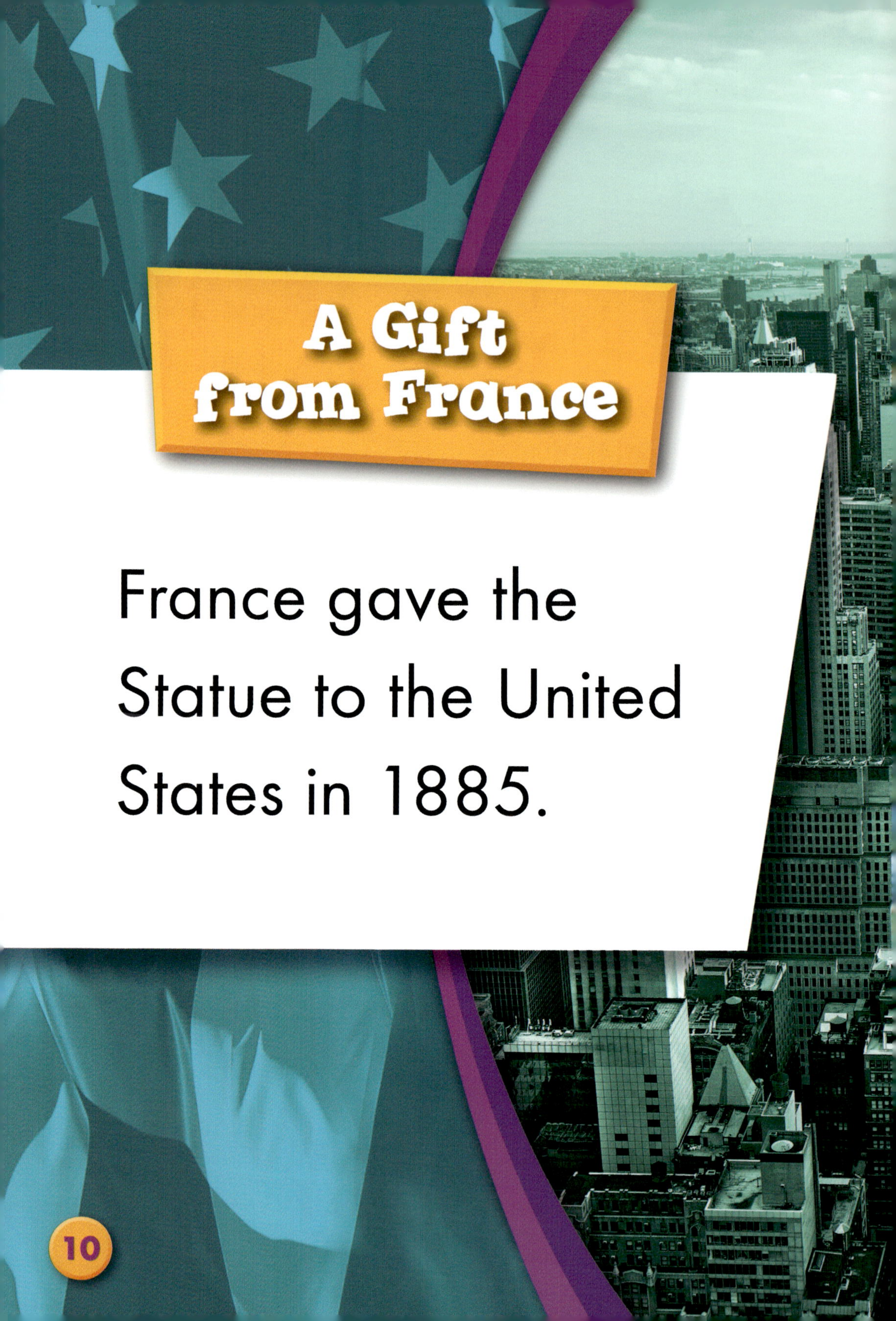

A Gift from France

France gave the Statue to the United States in 1885.

Traveling to the U.S.
France
United States

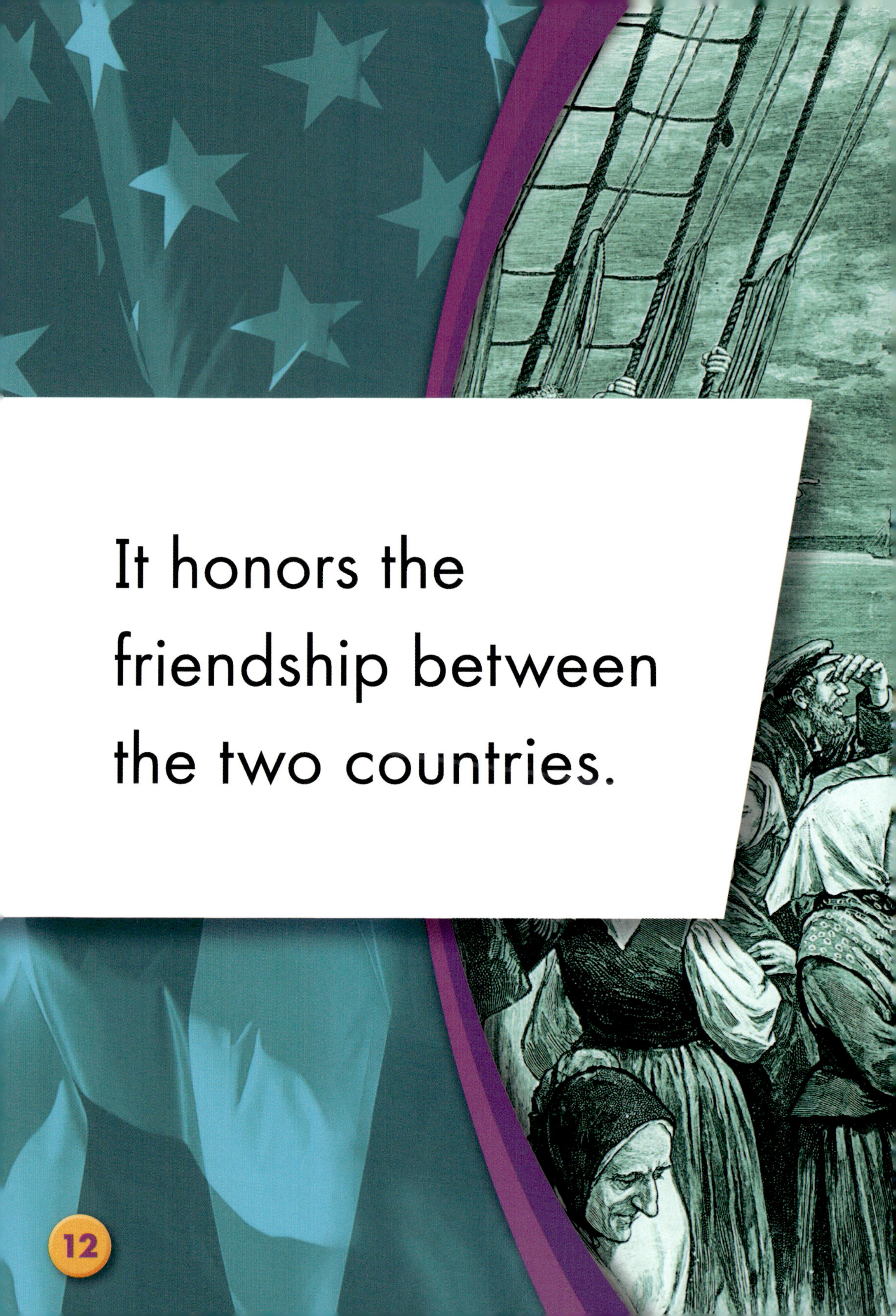

It honors the friendship between the two countries.

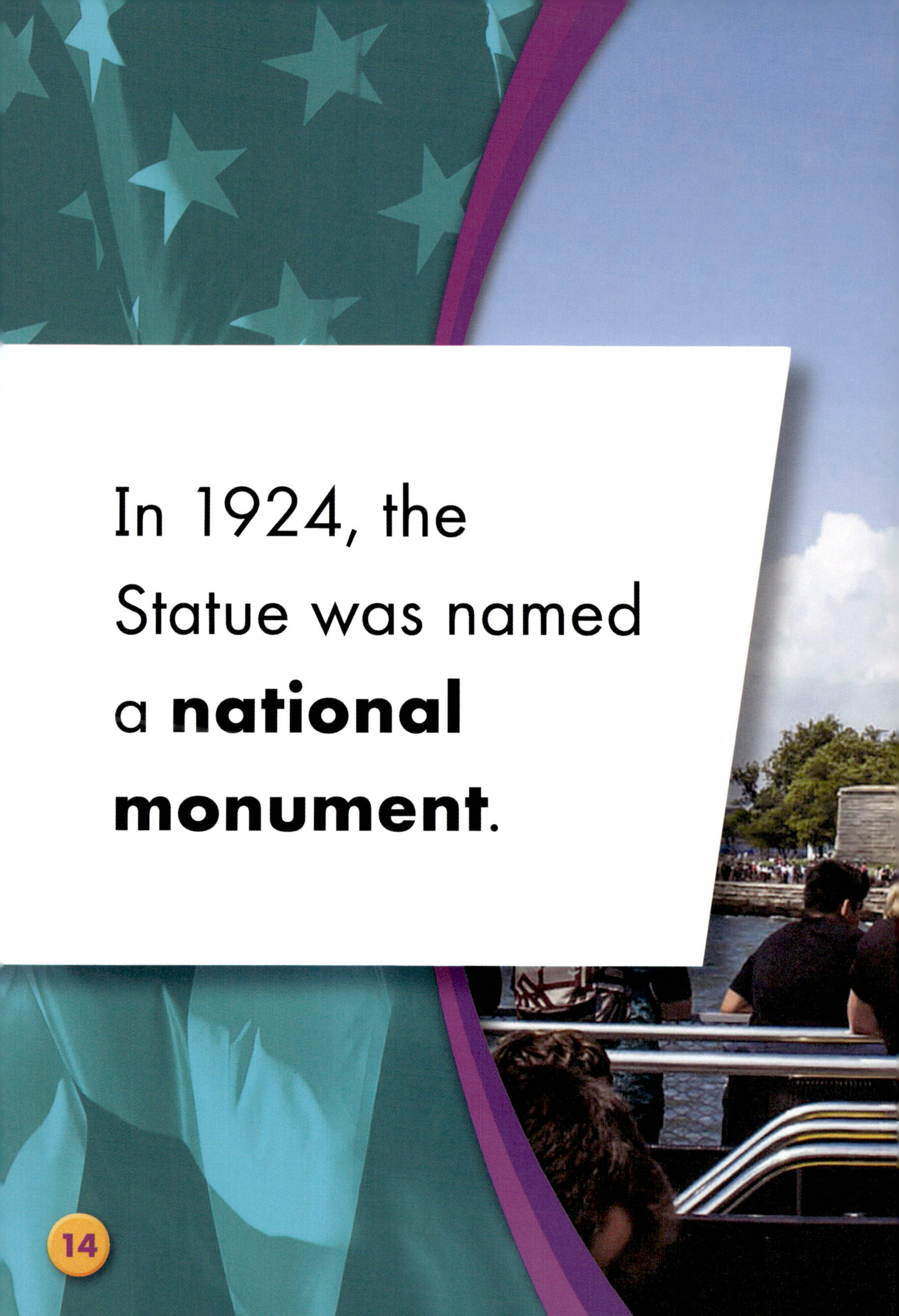

In 1924, the Statue was named a **national monument**.

Lady Liberty

The Statue holds a **torch**. It lights the way to **freedom**.

torch

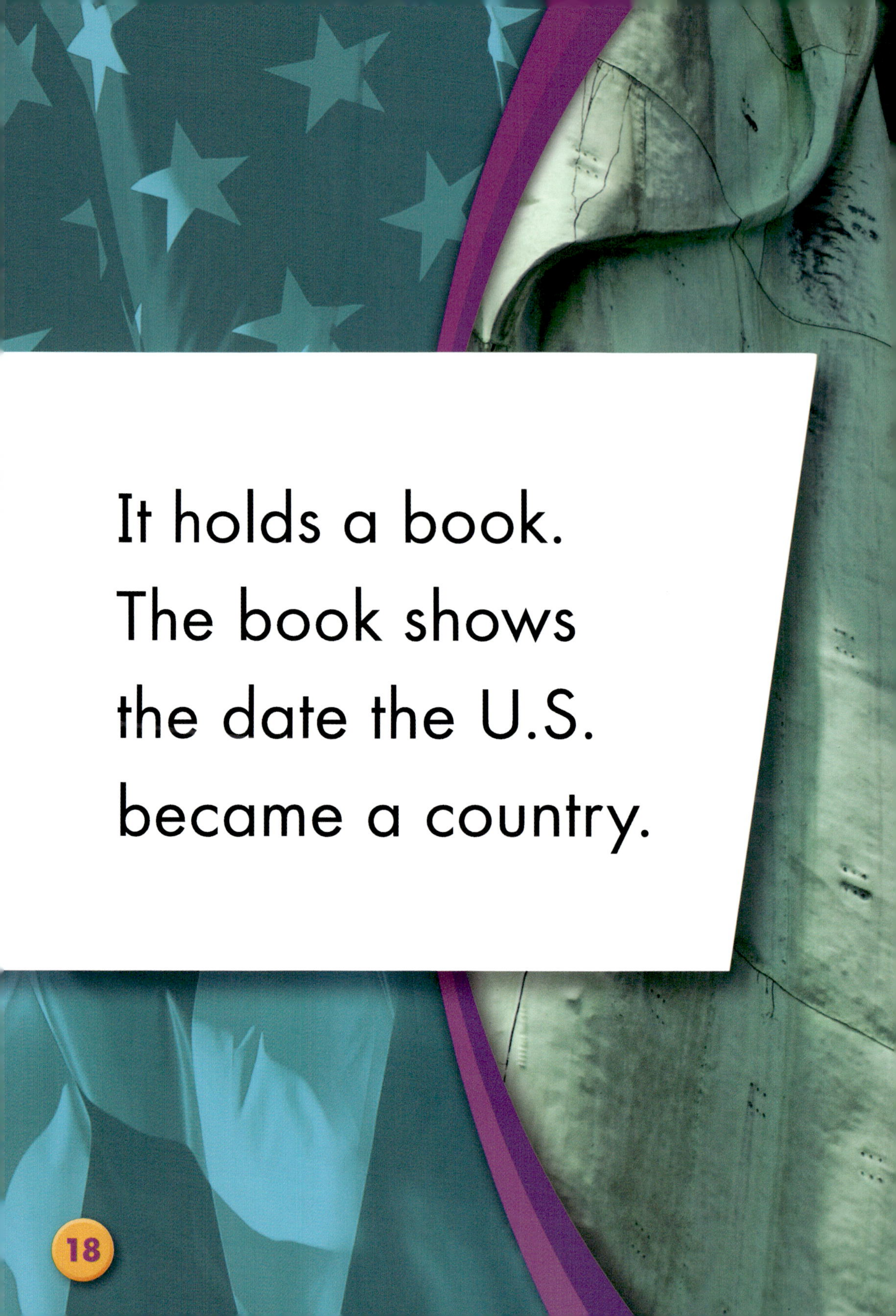

It holds a book. The book shows the date the U.S. became a country.

JULY
IV

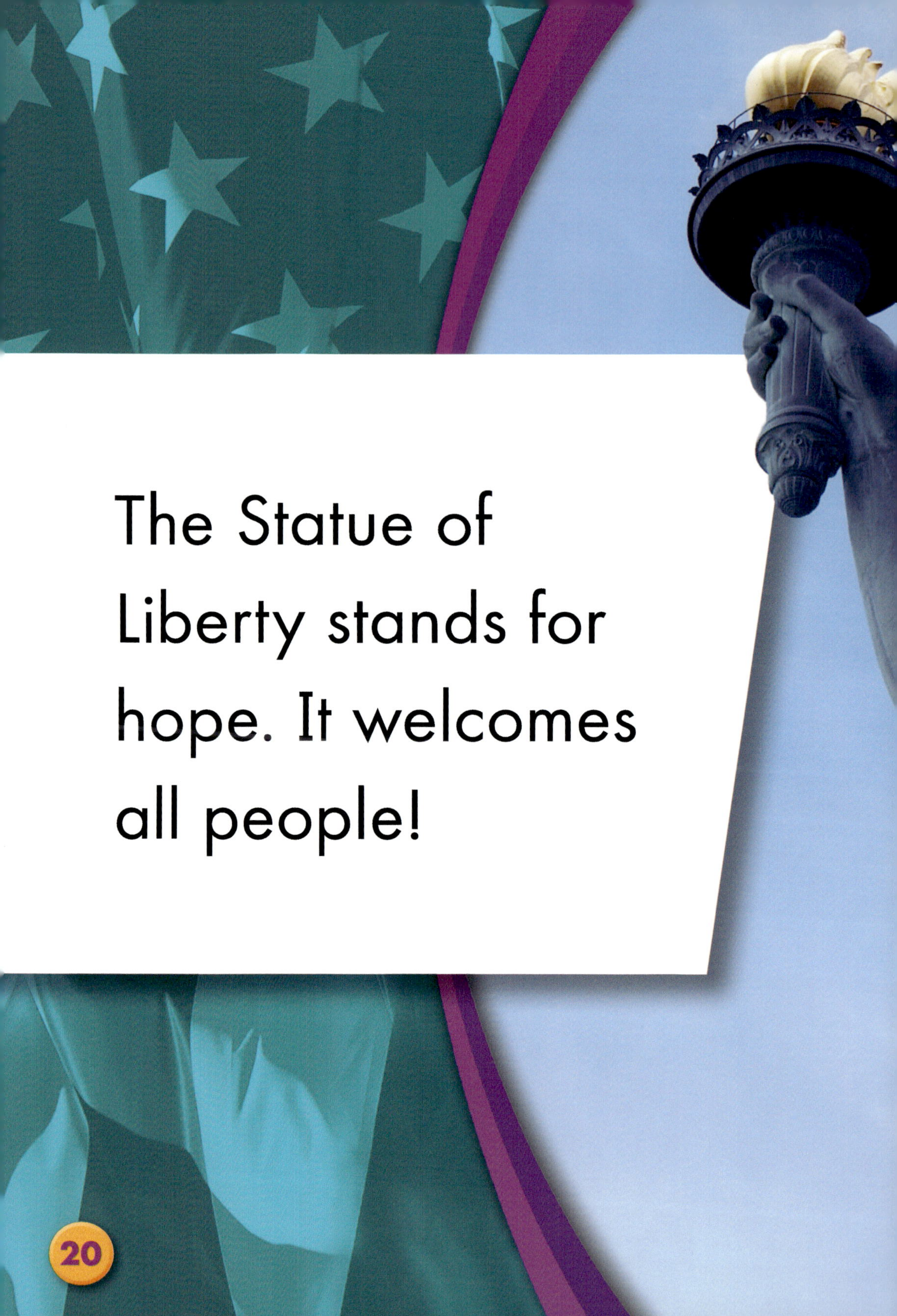

The Statue of Liberty stands for hope. It welcomes all people!

Glossary

democracy

a government in which the people choose their leaders

national monument

a statue or building that is important to the country

freedom

the state of being free

symbol

something that stands for something else

harbor

a part of the ocean or a lake that is next to land where ships are kept

torch

a small fire in a container that can be carried by hand

To Learn More

AT THE LIBRARY

Bailey, R.J. *Statue of Liberty.* Minneapolis, Minn.: Bullfrog Books, 2017.

Gaspar, Joe. *The Statue of Liberty.* New York, N.Y.: PowerKids Press, 2014.

Murray, Julie. *The Statue of Liberty.* Minneapolis, Minn.: Abdo Kids, 2017.

ON THE WEB

Learning more about the Statue of Liberty is as easy as 1, 2, 3.

1. Go to www.factsurfer.com.
2. Enter "Statue of Liberty" into the search box.
3. Click the "Surf" button and you will see a list of related web sites.

With factsurfer.com, finding more information is just a click away.

Index

The images in this book are reproduced through the courtesy of: Ismailciydem, front cover; Bildagentur Zoonar GmbH, p. 3; Felix Lipov, pp. 4-5; GagliardiImages, pp. 6-7; Bettmann/ Getty, pp. 8-9; Sergey Borisov/ Alamy, pp. 10-11; ventdusud, p. 11; bauhaus1000, pp. 12-13; littleny, pp. 14-15; stockpix4u, pp. 16-17; mathieukor, pp. 18-19; Tono Balaguer, pp. 20-21; NNut, p. 22 (top right); Inc, p. 22 (bottom right); fstop123, (middle left); Kit Leong, p. 22, (bottom left); vchal, p. 22 (top left); Monkey Business Images, p. 22 (middle right).